LITTLE MISS
SCATTER

sets off for the sun

Original concept by Roger Hargreaves
Illustrated and written by Adam Hargreaves

World International

Little Miss Scatterbrain is the sort of person who gets everything mixed up.

Like the morning she hung slices of bread from the washing line and put her handkerchiefs in the bread bin.

Like the afternoon she vacuumed the lawn and mowed the carpets.

And like the evening when she wanted to watch her favourite television programme, but turned on the radio instead.

Little Miss Scatterbrain is so scatterbrained that she forgets where her own front door is! Have you ever heard of anything so scatterbrained?

This story is about the time that she went on her summer holiday.

Little Miss Scatterbrain, as you can imagine, is not very good at organising holidays.

The year before last she went skiing, but ended up on the beach!

And last year she went camping and packed an electric kettle!

This year she was determined that nothing would go wrong.

And to make sure that nothing did go wrong she asked her friends to help her.

Mr Clever helped to book her summer holiday.

Little Miss Splendid helped her shop for her holiday.

Little Miss Tidy helped her pack.

Mr Rush took her to the station.

And Mr Strong carried her luggage onto the train.

Nothing could go wrong. Or that's what Little Miss Scatterbrain thought.

However, something did go wrong.

And that something was Little Miss Scatterbrain getting off at the wrong station.

She crossed the road and went into the hotel opposite the station.

"Good morning," she said, even though it was the afternoon, "my name is Miss Scatterbrain."

The hotel manager looked down his list of guests, but there was no booking in her name.

And of course there wouldn't be.

Little Miss Scatterbrain was in the wrong town. And because she was in the wrong town, she had to be in the wrong hotel.

"That's odd," she said, as she came out of the hotel. "Never mind, I'll go down to the beach."

She asked the next person she met where the beach was.

"Sorry, there's no beach here," came the reply.

"That's odd," she said for the second time that day.

As she stood in the street wondering what to do, somebody else walked by and said, "Looks like snow."

Miss Scatterbrain looked up at the sky and as she did, a large snowflake floated down and landed on her nose.

"That's odd," she said, for the third time that day.

A week later, back from her holiday, Little Miss Scatterbrain met Mr Clever.

"Hello," said Mr Clever. "Did you enjoy your holiday?"

"Yes," said Miss Scatterbrain, "do you want to see my photos?" And she showed Mr Clever her holiday snaps.

Not surprisingly, Mr Clever was rather surprised.

"That's odd. Where did you go?" he asked.

"It began with an 'S'," said Miss Scatterbrain.

"I know. I booked it for you," said Mr Clever. "You went to Seatown."

"No," said Miss Scatterbrain, "Hmmmm, let me think, oh, I know, it was Shivertown!"

"I should have guessed," smiled Mr Clever.

"By the way, did you get my postcard?"

"No, but I did get your postcard meant for Miss Splendid," chuckled Mr Clever.

"That's odd," said Miss Scatterbrain.

But I don't think there's anything odd about that, do you?!

3 Great Offers For Mr Men Fans

1 FREE Door Hangers and Posters

In every Mr Men and Little Miss Book like this one you will find a special token. Collect 6 and we will send you either a brilliant Mr. Men or Little Miss poster and a Mr Men or Little Miss double sided, full colour, bedroom door hanger. Apply using the coupon overleaf, enclosing six tokens and a 50p coin for your choice of two items.

Egmont World tokens can be used towards any other Egmont World / World International token scheme promotions., in early learning and story / activity books.

Posters: Tick your preferred choice of either Mr Men ☐ or Little Miss ☐

Door Hangers: Choose from: Mr. Nosey & Mr Muddle ☐, Mr Greedy & Mr Lazy ☐, Mr Tickle & Mr Grumpy ☐, Mr Slow & Mr Busy ☐, Mr Messy & Mr Quiet ☐, Mr Perfect & Mr Forgetful ☐, Little Miss Fun & Little Miss Late ☐, Little Miss Helpful & Little Miss Tidy ☐, Little Miss Busy & Little Miss Brainy ☐, Little Miss Star & Little Miss Fun ☐. (Please tick)

2 Mr Men Library Boxes

Keep your growing collection of Mr Men and Little Miss books in these superb library boxes. With an integral carrying handle and stay-closed fastener, these full colour, plastic boxes are fantastic. They are just £5.49 each including postage. Order overleaf.

3 Join The Club

To join the fantastic Mr Men & Little Miss Club, check out the page overleaf NOW!

Join Our Club!

MR. MEN & little Miss CLUB

When you become a member of the fantastic Mr Men and Little Miss Club you'll receive a personal letter from Mr Happy and Little Miss Giggles, a club badge with your name, and a superb Welcome Pack (pictured below right).

You'll also get birthday and Christmas cards from the Mr Men and Little Misses, 2 newsletters crammed with special offers, privileges and news, and a copy of the 12 page Mr Men catalogue which includes great party ideas.

If it were on sale in the shops, the Welcome Pack alone might cost around £13. But a year's membership is just £9.99 (plus 73p postage) with a 14 day money-back guarantee if you are not delighted!

HOW TO APPLY To apply for any of these three great offers, ask an adult to complete the coupon below and send it with appropriate payment and tokens (where required) to: Mr Men Offers, PO Box 7, Manchester M19 2HD. Credit card orders for Club membership ONLY by telephone, please call: 01403 242727.

To be completed by an adult

❏ 1. Please send a poster and door hanger as selected overleaf. I enclose six tokens and a 50p coin for post (coin not required if you are also taking up 2. or 3. below).

❏ 2. Please send __ Mr Men Library case(s) and __ Little Miss Library case(s) at £5.49 each.

❏ 3. Please enrol the following in the Mr Men & Little Miss Club at £10.72 (inc postage)

Fan's Name:_____Fan's Address:_____

_____

_____Post Code:_____Date of birth:___/___/___

Your Name:_____Your Address:_____

_____

Post Code:_____Name of parent or guardian (if not you):_____

Total amount due: £_____ (£5.49 per Library Case, £10.72 per Club membership)

❏ I enclose a cheque or postal order payable to Egmont World Limited.

❏ Please charge my MasterCard / Visa account.

Card number: | | | | | | | | | | | | | | | | |

Expiry Date: _____/_____   Signature: _____

Data Protection Act: If you do **not** wish to receive other family offers from us or companies we recommend, please tick this box ❏. Offer applies to UK only